MW00513568

D.A.N.T.E began his writing career with the horror/fantasy genre, crafting short stories. One of his short story collections includes *The Void Gospels*. These horror stories were focused on the conventional horror, fantasy and psychological elements. Setting ordinary people, who finds themselves in terrifying scenarios beyond their control. Most of D.A.N.T.E's works focused on the mysterious world known as 'Elseland,' breaking away the concept of reality between traditional horror and modern dark fantasy. The major influences to his work includes: Clive Barker, Stephen King, Dante Alighieri and H.P. Lovecraft.

To all who have believed in me.

D.A.N.T.E

THE VESSEL
OF ELSELAND

AUSTIN MACAULEY PUBLISHERS™

LONDON • CAMBRIDGE • NEW YORK • SHARJAH

A CIP catalogue record for this title is available from the British Library.

ISBN 9781398440265 (Paperback)
ISBN 9781398440272 (Hardback)
ISBN 9781398440289 (ePub e-book)

www.austinmacauley.com

First Published 2022
Austin Macauley Publishers Ltd®
1 Canada Square
Canary Wharf
London
E14 5AA

I am thanking the following people:

To my English tutor in East London, Angela Onelum, for revealing my potential.

My Maths tutor, Kasia Jarczewska, for her encouragement.

Prologue

Before there was time, before there was anything, there was nothing, and before there was nothing...there was Elseland.

Now fall, and know, my brave reader, that you are alone. There is only darkness for you and death for your people, if such a fate may be called death.

Our existence coming into your realm is only just the beginning. It is coming, and it will command the fabric of all reality. It will sail through into every world, every realm, until all that exists or shall ever exist will be extinguished. Sadly, my foolish reader, you are just a speck of flesh and blood compared to what your people would call us: gods and devils.

You already know that the end is coming, it is inevitable, and I am The All-Seeing.

So read on, reader. Read on if you dare – if you are brave enough – to know what is told in the text of the Void Gospels... The vessel of Elseland.

I

The Unknown Artist

There wasn't a moment or a word to describe when or how this story sprang into motion. No origin for this space of cold, grey, brick walls. Nothing occupied the space but Dante, sitting – since it's all he could do – on the floor. Such a room, so airtight that nothing, not even the sound of a fly or the gentle breeze, could disturb his isolation. With his knees levelling up to his face, the eyes of this young man fiercely stare ahead of him. How odd, the object of his stare: a calendar, it would appear, hanging up on the wall in front of him. Curiosity building up in his subconsciousness, Dante slowly stands and approaches it.

Dante observes a vintage swimsuit calendar that appears to be from the 1980s. How fortunate for Dante: this month has one of his favourite actors, Linda Blair. Looking more closely at the date, May 2018, Dante knows it can't be right. When did the actress posed for this shot?

His senses warn him that something isn't quite right around here. The thoughts of this young man spring into action. His attention is easily broken and quickly moves to something else.

A voice echoes towards him, speaking in a ghostly tone that cannot be described as even close to human:

'Dante.'

The voice, naturally bubbly, creates the impression of seductive giggling. How eerie that this voice should speak in some unearthly language and yet Dante can understand it quite clearly. The young man turns his head to discover where the unknown voice could be coming from, unaware of what lies ahead.

With shattering force, numerous strange arms pierces through the walls as if they were cardboard. Dante quickly turns away, but it is too late; the arms have reached out to him.

***

His reaction to what has just passed before his eyes awakes him to the real world and alerts the person sitting next to him world.

'Whoa, easy! You okay, Dante?' Jim wants to know.

Now Dante is aware that he is in the back seat of a London taxi, accompanied by his friend, Jim Crowley – a fellow artist and quite possibly his closest friend in the art world.

At last, he gathers his bearings and realizes where he is. Glimpses of his intense experience, which felt so real to him, slowly begin to fade away.

'Yeah, I'm fine,' Dante answers, 'just worried that you were going to try and suck me off.'

Jim looks unsurprised by his friend's foul remark. 'Well,' he says with a sigh, 'at least you're in a good mood for a change.'

Now the taxi is driving through the busy traffic of the City of London, passing by Euston Square and heading in the direction of King's Cross St Pancras.

'Do I really have to go?' Dante moans, 'No one would ever notice if I'm there or not.'

'Dante,' Jim says, wanting to get through to him, 'just try and talk to some people. You never know...'

'I fucking hate people.' But his appearance does not match this sour expression.

'You might meet a nice redhead,' Jim teases him.

'Redhead, you say?'

Neither could help but laugh spontaneously at Dante's personal interest.

The taxi makes a final turn, and there it is: the crypt where their art show is being held, along with that of eight other artists. There's a bump under the wheels, followed by the sound of the taxi slowing down over pebbled ground. Now the vehicle comes to a complete stop outside the entrance to the crypt.

'That's £26 for the fare,' the taxi driver says.

Jim pays the fare because Dante cannot. Sadly, the young artist's fortunes are such that paying for a simple cab fare has become a luxury for him.

'Have fun, Banksy,' the driver deliberately mocks Dante before slowly driving away.

Dante is standing with Jim as the car leaves their sight. Alas, the poor artist felt the insult as a blunt knife jabbing deep into his chest. Jim, on the other hand, did not hear the driver's comment as an insult, or that it was directed at Dante.

Time is upon them. Both are checked on the guest list, and down the steps they go. To the sound of music and chattering of people, they enter the crypt.

***

Dante knows the true faces of those he can see around him. Indeed, they are poorly hidden. They would simply walk through him as if he were a ghost. He could, of course, make the first move and introduce himself, tolerating the idle chit-chat intended to humour the artist rather than acknowledging his worth. Dante's eyes see nothing but spectacular certainties. It is no brainteaser where he can find his artwork. Hardly surprising that it is displayed far back within the crypt, easily missed in the dim light, so that it can be forgotten in time. There is no debating it now: presenting himself to this show was a goddamn mistake; some may call it a premonition or déjà vu. In time, those he would refer to as "regular dildos" would start to come out of the woodwork. And so it begins. Many have already started to humour him. In their minds, they refer to him as 'simple,' assuming that Dante is not aware of their mockery of his intelligence.

'Oh look, it's Dante!' Borat points him out and turns his head towards Jamie, the director of the Sling-guns Gallery, who is unable to avoid interacting with the frustrated artist.

It is all Jamie can do to politely acknowledge Dante. Without so much as a 'Hello' or even an effort to make eye-contact, all he does is give the clichéd awkward handshake, as if he does not know how to shake a person's hand. The director does not care much for Dante. Fortunately for Jamie, the artist decides to avoid any drama and plays along, quietly shaking his hand.

Desperate to find his friend, Dante quickly manages to find Jim and is reunited with the only person he can tolerate inside this crypt. Jim's popularity means that all Dante can do is act as a human shadow, standing patiently until he can catch up socially with him, reminiscing about old times. Following Jim around, no one seems to realize Dante is there. He may as well be wearing an invisible cloak.

The complete rejection of social interaction leaves Dante free to occupy himself with the display of tombstones and coffins. How eerie! Yet he feels the additional strange sense of something unnatural brush by his skin, raising goosebumps. He cannot help but look in its direction and catches sight of a naked woman walking through the crowd. Dante can find no words to accurately describe her strange form. Her features are a phenomenon, almost monstrous and yet so absolutely beautiful that his eyes cannot turn away. The woman is something far beyond human.

'Did you see that?'

'See what?'

Dante is puzzled by Jim's response. He should know what Dante is talking about.

'That w—' Dante points to where the woman is.

Or at least where she should be. The strange woman has vanished without a trace. There is much for the artist's to process: did he hallucinate her, or perhaps he has reached a point where he is heading towards a mental breakdown.

In the midst of his confusion, sown by the recent bizarreness, the sudden intrusion of an unwelcoming voice interrupts Dante's train of thought:

'Dante,' Liam obnoxiously mocks him, 'I fucking love your artwork. It's just like Basquiat.'

Yeah, and? goes through Dante's mind, narrating what he wishes he could have said. Sadly, he misses the opportunity to point out to Liam that he is missing the whole point of his work.

But it doesn't matter; he would never fully notice art, nor Dante's talents. And so, Liam continues to ramble on and on about the comparison to another artist's work, rather than appreciating what the artist was trying to achieve.

As time moves on, more and more it keeps growing, this gathering of people filling up the crypt. The opening night of the show has proved to be a smash for all art lovers. But it would have been better for Dante if he were somehow more involved, able to connect with the energized atmosphere around him.

Nothing stops these guests coming, swarming into the crypt like cockroaches going into a roach motel. Thoughts of the people that Dante was hoping to avoid soon increase and become more difficult to dismiss. Sadly, one such person gives the artist cause to sigh. Now the predictable routine begins.

Miles is standing, of all places in the crypt, next to Dante's artwork. It would surprise people to know that this man Dante hopes to avoid is his art dealer from the Antelope Gallery. Despite his great reputation, the artist has never been too fond of him. Dante has barely sold one piece through him over the last four years, placing him deep into financial desperation. Fortunately for Miles, the artist chooses to endure the ramblings of his art dealer, telling stories to two young ladies that were walking by, although it leaves a bitter aftertaste on Dante's tongue as he is forced to watch this sad display.

'I've sold 12–13 of his pieces this year.' Miles pressures the artist, 'huh, Dante?'

Now looking at Miles, the artist knows that he has no choice.

'Yeah…' Dante says with such coldness.

If the claims made by Miles were even close to the truth, then why is Dante so deep in financial despair, so depressed that he has to degrade himself, stooping so low as to tolerate such abuse, praying that someday he will break through this shitstorm.

'Tell me again, Miles,' Dante surprises him, 'which pieces did we sell recently?'

Putting Miles on the spot, he hopes to expose the pathological liar. A perfect payback after crossing the artist too many times.

'You're so funny, Dante,' Miles laughs.

Unbearable. Dante looks for the ideal opportunity to get away from Miles. With poor timing, Andy – Borat's boyfriend, one more that Dante was hoping to avoid – stops him. Unable to escape from Andy's orbit, once more Dante counts down to the expected conversation. *In three, two, one…*

'Remember when you had that solo show?' Andy looks at the young artist with eyes filled with pity for him.

Annoyance starts to cloud over the artist's head.

'It was years ago,' Andy says. 'No one showed up and you were very upset.' He smiles, 'So I came to it.'

While the self-flattery continues, poor Dante tries to push down his emotions, quite unimpressed by Andy's predictable view of himself, and so tired of being looked at like some sad, broken, pathetic little puppy. Andy wouldn't even have known about the show if Dante hadn't announced it to him.

And so, as his eyes glaze over, Dante takes in the socialising now taking place. The scene is familiar from many gatherings: a line has formed, queuing up for a selfie with Borat, who is claiming that he is some kind of legend. Of course, amidst the many involved in this selfie frenzy, Dante – who, to others, is seen as nothing but a transparent object – is excluded. It is clear that his instinct was correct; coming here was a mistake.

Being alone in this crowd starts to weigh heavily on his fragile ego, so the artist moves towards Jim. The sounds of laughter; people smiling all around the fortunate Jim – so admired, respected, and even loved by many; it is a beautiful image, one that Dante has longed for. Inside the mind of the troubled artist are voices of realisation that this world of success and respect will never be within the grasp of his fingertips: a balloon too high for a child to reach as it floats into the great sky.

Such a high level of insecurity amongst his close circle of friends is nothing out of the ordinary for poor Dante, and he is not afraid to admit it. On many occasions, his defence mechanism would kick in, referring to his respected friend as "Bitch-boy" or "My girlfriend". Despite how much he hates it, demeaning Jim from time to time is the only way he can cope with the sharp pain of his insecurity. All of this is due to the damage caused by others: according to them, he is nothing more than a bad joke; they treat him with pity and regard him as some form of charity. Never have they looked at him for his worth. Never have they appreciated his talent and creative mind. But they do not see how easily Dante can see through them.

Placing himself in a cobweb-filled corner, standing all alone, Dante watches. The infection of modern technology is revealed in the desperate need of so many to record every moment through selfies on their phones. Dante goes unnoticed by the growing number of people, who pass him by as if he does not exist. What a shame, at the end of the night, that everyone has missed the great opportunity to meet an artist of such talent, someone who could soar high into the heavens: a true gift from God. But then, why should they care?

After all, who gives a shit about Dante?

II

The Realm of Sweet Dreams

Oh, what a heavenly delight! Yet it is nothing but a natural, white light shining through the window of a country house. A brightened delight that shines with such happiness and peace, covering the surface of a red carpet. These rays of sunshine reveal the room as a bedroom for a child: a young boy, it would seem. Such sweetness in the air that shares the joy, the fondness of this child, lying quietly on the floor with smiles of ambition and his eyes filled with dreams. The sound of the coloured pencil upon the surface of the paper, bringing his imagination to life. This time of great joy passes, and the red carpet is gradually covered by layers of scattered paper. Each drawing reveals the boy's passion and obsession for creating. This is nothing but a pleasant memory that fills a person's soul with such innocence. The griping harshness that is known as reality will soon break through the fairy-tale sound of chirping birds.

'Dante!' the man screams at him. 'Hey, Banksy,' he says, 'get ya head outta the fucking clouds.'

***

Now he has awoken from his pleasant dream of some faraway memory, all thoughts gradually return to the "gripping" reality that is his life: the story of the troubled artist, unable to make a living from his art, forced to work in a minimum-wage job. Dante, standing outside the Beatrice Tate School, painting its gates, quietly turns and faces the man who yelled at him: his unpleasant boss, Shital.

'You're not painting a mural, you know,' Shital mocks.

'I want to do this right. It's gotta be perfect,' Dante replies.

'Doing it right, doing it right, that's always your excuse. It's a goddamn gate!' His boss waves angrily. 'You spent over an hour on these bars already!'

The young artist cannot ignore the hostile behaviour of his boss, so he stops painting.

'You don't understand,' he says. 'None of you has ever understood. I'm an artist.' He speaks so proudly.

'No, what you are is fired, shithead!'

Dante drops his paintbrush in surprise.

'Wai— You can't…' He pleads against the decision of his unfair boss.

'I just did.' Shital speaks so coldly.

Dante's panic level rises. He really needs this job and Shital is quite aware of the fact. The young artist begs to him to reconsider, but clearly his boss does not care and shows no form of compassion for him as he walks away. Dante struggles to process what has just happened. He was unprepared for this turn of events. Of course, the relationship between the artist and his now former boss had not been an easy one from the very start. From the day Dante first worked for the company, Shital had never shown any trust or confidence in this hard-working artist. Many memories of such negativity lurk upon Dante. Not once had Shital praised or appreciated his hard work, yet how puzzling that Dante's colleagues and, oddly, the other supervisors should have praised so much of his work.

Now what goes through his mind is panic, fear and this important question: what is he going to do now that he is out of a job?

***

A thunderstorm broods over the colourful area that is known as Brick Lane. Even Mother Nature herself won't give Dante a break tonight. Inside Monty's Bar, Shoreditch's popular hangout – especially for local artists – it appears to be a quiet night, which is quite unusual. But for Dante, it's exactly the atmosphere he wants. Now sitting by the bar, he quietly listens to the barmaid, who is sharing her concerns regarding a dear friend of hers.

'Jesus, that sucks!' Staring into his empty glass, Dante acknowledges the barmaid while he is trying to figure out his own problems.

'Yeah, I feel worst for his wife and kids,' she replies.

Dante's focus on the conversation of the barmaid that he has known for years is soon broken by an unfamiliar voice:

'At least he has a wife and kids.'

It is grim, dark, with the eeriness of something not human: a voice of some unknown origin. What language is this? Nothing of this world. Dante has never heard such words, yet somehow, he is able to understand them. With unsettled feelings of curiosity about such a voice and, more terrifyingly,

21

to whom it may belong, the artist turns in its direction. And there it is, sitting in the far back of the bar, hidden in darkness, the origin of this voice: it is a twisted-shaped figure, far too surreal and inhuman to be of this earth. Dante struggles to find words to adequately describe this figure: a man made of shadows, a shadow man. Dante has selected the perfect name: the Shadow Man.

'What have you got, Dante?' The Shadow Man speaks, looking directly at the artist with eyes of emptiness, taunting at him with remarks of maleficence. 'No job, no money, a life wasted, now all gone past your reach.' His laughter echoes directly into Dante's soul, slicing him as if with razor blades.

'Shut up!' rages Dante. 'You don't know a goddamn thing about me!' he screams.

Understandably, this outburst of aggression begins to draw the concerned attention of many. The barmaid responds immediately, approaching the artist's sudden behaviour with caution, there being no obvious cause for it. outburst. Dante's eyes now widen to the realisation that he is screaming at nothing. It takes a while for his mind to return to reason, then he knows what he must do: Dante turns to the barmaid and quickly apologies. He is in no doubt that he has overstayed his welcome, and, without a second thought, he gets off his stool and quietly leaves the bar.

The blackest night of crashing thunder breaks all silence. Dante now walks through the streets of Whitechapel, trapped in his trance of worries. He stumbles back home in a zombified state, oblivious to any noise of obnoxious drunkenness. As the night progresses, it is clear that nothing waits for him.

The sounds from outside barely break through the walls of this council building, located in Tower Hamlets. And there he is, coming out of the storm and entering into the gloomy hallway of depression. Sadly, this is where Dante is currently living: an old, crumbling structure, neglected by the eyes and untouched by modern hands. An ideal place for the forgotten souls that society has given up on whose minds are filled with nothing but troubling concerns. This poor artist is no exception as he walks through these corridors, accompanied only by the shroud of darkness and dim lights around him.

As he reaches his door, Dante just stands there, eyes glazed, the sound of keys jingling, and his mind becomes unfocused so that he cannot open the door. Finding the correct key proves too much of a struggle for him. Stressed and tired, he gives up easily and, frustrated, slowly crouches to the floor. So distressed at how shitty his life has become, he stares towards his door, knowing that tomorrow will be no different. Now, as he places his head against the wall behind him, he closes his eyes, inhales deeply, and wonders why he should go on.

'You know' – a woman speaks – 'sitting like that isn't good for your back.'

Not looking towards the speaker, Dante replies, 'Wouldn't be the worst.'

'Shitty day, huh?' she asks.

Dante slowly opens his eyes and, without any enthusiasm, he turns and looks at the speaker: a red-headed woman, wearing black, with ocean-blue eyes that you could easily get lost in. He is completely mesmerised by her beauty and is speechless, barely any words escaping from the artist's mouth.

Aware of his stammering, the woman smiles and crouches down, looking at him, eyes level with his:

I said, 'Shitty day?'

'U-uh— Yeah,' he mumbles, 'I got fired today...'

'That sucks,' she says.

'No,' he responds, 'I mean— It's good, now I can focus on my art.'

The woman smirks, 'Let me guess. Struggling artist. Couldn't have picked an obvious cliché, huh?'

Dante pauses, realising how right she is. 'Yeah...' he chuckles.

Aware that this mysterious woman is influencing the artist, nevertheless he cannot help but be drawn to her.

'Wow, your...' He pauses.

'Yeah,' she encourages.

'There's something about you...'

Dante is trying to find the right words, but the redhead knows what he's trying to ask:

'You saying you want to paint me?'

'He's saying he wants to take you inside and fuck your brains out.' Some strange, eerie voice speaks near Dante.

But it is not the Shadow Man who is appearing in the physical plane, but another of Dante's personal demons: a female, her monstrous form similar to the Shadow Man, yet unmatched by the even darkest imagination. The head of this creature is impaled by some strange, unnatural metal rods, which appear to be surgically hooked to the back of the skull, crudely attached like a canvas to a frame.

'No,' the artist panics, 'it's not like that!'

The red-headed woman looks puzzled. No one else is here, so how can Dante be talking to?

'Like what?' she asks quirkily.

Dante sighs with relief that he didn't scare the woman away and reminds himself not to let the demons overpower him.

The redhead cannot help but giggle, finding the artist's behaviour odd, but adorable.

'I gotta go…' she smiles and gets up and slowly heads towards the front entrance.

'Bu— Will I…,' Dante mutters to her.

The red-headed woman stands by the door and, slowly turning her head, she smiles at him.

'See ya around, tiger.' And, just like that, she was gone, out of the door.

Dante, now standing, stares towards the door. He questions whether he will ever see the red-headed woman again, or whether she has walked out of his life. Wonders if their paths will ever cross again. And in that moment the female demon reappears.

'Translation – "Fuck. Off. Loser."' The whisper comes from behind his ear.

The artist tilts his head down, knowing the demon is right. As his depression sinks in, one thing comes to mind: who would ever be interested in him?

As the creaking door opens, Dante can do nothing but stand there in his flat, a dark, cupboard-sized property with walls old and chipped, revealing the brickwork underneath. Barely a spot of dim light reveals the surroundings of screaming depression. Alas, his home is nothing but a storage room – in fact, more of a museum, filled with thirteen years

25

of his artwork, thirteen years of failure. Every last piece of his artwork is coated with dust, evidence that no collector would dare own any of it. Truly, this is a place abandoned of all hope, filled with despair.

His eyes are filled with such loathing, so little does he want to be here. Finally, he drags himself further inside the flat. Dante is nothing but a shell of his former self. A match for his home, he is no longer filled with hope or determination as he approaches his tattered old couch. Here he is, hidden in the dim, natural state of night, staring into the blank white canvas displayed on an easel in front of him.

'Aw, poor Dante.' The Shadow Man speaks. 'How are you going to pay the rent now?' he mocks. 'It's not too late, you know, to give all this up.'

These words of the Shadow Man pierce into Dante and the harsh reality of his struggles.

'It's their fucking fault!' the artist yells. 'If they ju—'

'Always someone else's fault,' the Shadow Man interrupts, 'never yours. Pathetic.'

Dante does not speak, just pauses, realising how right the Shadow Man is: such harshness, and yet his words speak honestly of his failures.

As the night progresses, the artist begins his routine of preparation, his ritual to drown out his self-loathing: heating the spoon and, with the flick of a long needle, injecting the heroin into his right arm, relieving him from his troubled mind. How far Dante has fallen, needing to use this dangerous substance to cope with his reality. Soon, he begins to drift into a sense of peace, reaching a level of high where he can escape his problems. But, in time, the high will fade and Dante will have to face reality again. For now, the troubled artist is sleeping in his bed, hoping such pleasant dreams will leave him with a better light of positivity. As his eyes gently shut and his face assumes a state of peaceful calm, he drifts into the land of slumber.

***

His eyes open to the sudden breeze of unfamiliar air. Somehow, Dante has awoken to a place that is not of Earth. Warily, he observes that he is not even in his own bed, but a European-style bed with wood engraving detail. A bed fit for a king in ancient times. The bedsheet, something that a giant could sleep under, has a wonderful texture. The touch of it upon Dante's skin: such unimaginable comfort and silkiness. This bedsheet can't be man-made, but unearthly and almost nightmarish simultaneously. What marvels are these? Dante has experienced nothing that compares with where he has woken. A world— A world beyond anything else. How can something feel so cold that it can reach into your soul and be simultaneously hellish and heavenly? The landscape and sky resemble something from a bad 90s music video: badly designed CGI, and colours beyond any human experience.

Is this a dream, or a horrifying truth that he does not want to acknowledge?

Dante becomes aware of unnatural, voice-like echoes, oddly similar to his personal demons, an unearthly and peculiar language, but one that he can understand. The echoes carry a sense of arousing desire that cries out sexual lust. Slow and deep breathing with a touch of gentle giggling. Dante cannot help but be curious, and slightly aroused.

A sudden movement of the sheet that lays over the bed causes Dante's eyes to swiftly turn to see an oddly shaped, almost human-sized bulge slowly rising from underneath the sheet. Dante stares, fearful, without moving a muscle. The bulge emerges through the sheet without making a tear. How can this be possible? The sheet behaves as if it were liquid.

Now the form of the bulge finally reveals itself: a slim woman, posing on all fours like an animal. She is completely naked, and her presence carries a strange aura of unimaginably seductive power. This unknown woman is nothing close to human, with skin closely resembling blue, and yet not blue. She is bald, with lusty lips that you want to kiss. Her eyes are cold, filled with darkness and yet with an appetite for the flesh of man. Any man or woman would be aroused and horrified at the same time by the body of this strange creature. Ah, sweet God, she's the envy of many for her figural beauty. And yet her body is covered by mutilations, exposing her flesh and bone – were these intentional, or from birth? She is both a sculpture of paradise and the stuff of nightmares.

Never before has this artist been so paralysed, hypnotised. Is it caused by this beautiful creature of feminine perfection? In a sight most terrifying, she begins to slowly crawl towards Dante, with eyes of sexual hunger for him.

Dante never expected, nor can he avoid this strange presence. And it is just the beginning. Dante's eyes are now drawn to his left foot, where, slowly, another bulge rises from under the sheet. Just like the first, it emerges through the sheet without making a tear, revealing itself to be another woman with appearances so nearly identical to the other that they could be twins.

So now there are two of them. Sisters, it seems. They both crawl closer to him with eyes of identical motive. Closer and closer, they tower over him and the artist cannot avoid the sight of their beauty, their large, perfect breasts. There is nothing else Dante can see to explain their sexual appetite. They lower themselves close to his body, squishing their soft, silky breasts onto his chest, filling their breath with excitement and slowly exhaling from deep within their mouths. These twins, cruel in their playful attempt to taunt and tease the artist simply by the movement of their lips – slow, and barely touching the top of Dante's chest – reach up to his neck, turning him weak and yet yearning for more.

Dante feels the slight, soft touch of their claw-like nails on his body as they gently nibble upon his earlobes and their hands caress his chest. The twin on his right moves her lips to his, and both passionately engage in a lip lock. The artist cannot control himself, almost hypnotised, and submits to her lustful beauty. It isn't long before the other twin feels left out, wanting a taste of Dante's lips herself. Such a sensation, overwhelmed by their sensitive nipples rubbing against his, causes Dante to engage their burning lustfulness with his tongue, struggling to keep up with theirs. Both want the artist, and they are all that he wants.

Once more, the twin on the right makes her move, slowly moving her hand, gently stroking his skin until her nails reach the side of his chest. Whether to mimic this action, or by some telepathic link, her sister simultaneously does the same with her hand, and now both will introduce Dante beyond the limits of sex. The air fills with the sound of lust as both sisters slowly sink their fingers under his armpit as if into putty, gradually moving their hands under his chest and gently caressing the flesh and bone beneath Dante's skin. Thus the true power of these twin sisters is revealed, making the artist powerless to stop them as they touch him, want him. And of course, he wants the twins for himself. Why should he not? Why should he try to resist? If these are devils, what can angels possibly be like? Truly, this must be what Heaven is.

Dante is nothing but putty in their hands, allowing the fingers of these two lustful ladies to gently stroke every nerve, every muscle and every organ inside him. The movement under the skin that caresses the aroused artist is such that he feels he is reaching something that surpasses the human orgasm. Is he reaching a new level that is far beyond the senses of pain and pleasure? No doubt Dante is beyond absolute bliss. He wishes he would climax right now.

He is already far beyond anything he thought he could take when another bulge begins to take shape. Could it be that these twins are not the only ones who are drawn to Dante? This one is rising between his legs, stretching up high under the sheet like a ghost, before slowly sliding through it as the others had done. As the sheet returns to its original form, the figure is revealed, placed on top of Dante's crotch.

It is another strange woman, this one quite different from the twins: her body is flawless and toned, so powerful and yet overwhelmingly desirable. The colour of her skin is almost golden, suggesting a divine presence. She appears to have a gauntlet on her right arm, monstrous and deadly with claws that are the stuff of nightmares. The woman's figure does not appear mutilated like the others, but her ribcage is exposed underneath her soft, but firm breasts. Oh wow, she has the face of noble beauty, yet with eyes that appear to be the portal of Hell.

30

There is no hesitation and, as she stares directly at Dante, she slowly strokes her hands upon his abdomen and places herself onto his member, penetrating deep inside her.

So fierce is the expression of her sexual engagement, the slow movement of her hips and heavy breathing. Oh God, such hunger, such animal rawness expressed by the grinding of her lower teeth. As for Dante, he is completely overwhelmed by this woman and her large appetite for his manhood, needing him, wanting him, the craving of her own flesh. Her craving becomes more aggressive. She grabs the artist's hands and places them firmly upon her breasts, thrusting her hips more and more as Dante's pleasure deepens.

Tension now begins to draw towards Dante. This beautiful creature of lust may be physically too much for him to handle. He squeezes her breasts tightly. He wants her as she wants him, truly a sexual demon with unlimited desire.

The twins will not be stopped from having their fun, slowly moving their hands from underneath Dante's skin, moving up to his face as if his body were truly made of silky putty. The long fingers ripple under Dante's face – stroking, caressing, touching every inch of his skull, overwhelming the senses far beyond human comprehension. But none of this is enough for the twins, who cannot be satisfied. They move their lips so close to his cheeks, giggling with excitement, before they lock their own tongues together, acting more like passionate lovers than sisters.

Faster and faster, the golden woman thrusts harder with the pleasure of him inside her, almost to the point of climax. Rubbing her hands towards the chest of the artist, her long fingers begin to sink in, just like those of the twins, until her whole hands are inside, gripping onto him, able to truly feel him as she comes close to satisfaction. Harder and harder she thrusts herself, up and down, breathing heavily in sync with him. What joy she is having. Truly, she is a sexual creature who acts however she pleases. She behaves as if she has been waiting centuries for his throbbing manhood. A sight of unimaginable wildness, these strange women and their insatiable lust, their fierce yearning and appetite for a man's flesh.

Dante cannot last much longer. His spirit is willing, but his body is not that of a god. The repeated pattern of moans and deep breaths tells him that such animal hunger may finally be reaching satisfaction. This primal form of mating has lasted so long, it is as if centuries have passed. The golden woman thrusts harder and harder to the point where it is just too much for all four of them. So close to the point where the echoing sounds of these women will peak to absolute orgasm...

Then Dante awakes in a cold sweat and returns to the land of the living. Many questions about what has occurred reach his mind: was it a dream, or was it something more? He notices the thick, wet stickiness upon his right palm.

III

Human Nature

Through the chaos of travel within the City of London, deep underground inside the Northern tube line, our unlucky artist now journeys onwards to the Antelope Gallery in Camden.

Dante's history can be read in the expression of unhappiness on his face as he now stands within the tightening space of the surrounding crowd. He knows that soon he will be getting off at his destination, aware of how few options he's got left. Of course, this will not stop him from attending the meeting, but he knows it will bring nothing but mockery for him.

An hour has passed, and he's now at his stop. Footsteps sound as Dante walks up these pillars of stairs. The natural light of daytime reaches the artist's eyes as he exits Camden Station into the crowd of loud noise. The development of his anxiety has nothing to do with being surrounded by strangers, but in knowing that the gallery is now not too far away. Even the busy and bright colours of positive beauty that fill this place cannot bring the young artist any happiness. Indeed, as he walks on through these streets, dragging his feet like a zombie, he is unable to admire the beauty of these sights. Dante heads in the direction of Chalk Farm, passing by the

Roundhouse Theatre and closer, towards the costume shop near Sainsbury's. In but a moment and a simple walk around the corner, Dante has reached his destination. As he is stands outside the Antelope Gallery, he wishes this moment hadn't come so quickly. His frozen stillness is filled with nothing but discomfort, knowing that he will soon have to enter inside. Dante's eyes catch a glimpse through the glass window, seeing another art dealers, Annabelle De'Ville, inside.

There is nothing the artist can do now but take a deep breath and... Just before he opens the door, he hesitates.

'It's not too late Dante,' the Shadow Man whispers. 'There's still time. You can walk away,' he says. 'There is always a career serving coffee.'

Dante takes another deep breath and exhales as he tries to drown out the demon. Now, he slowly turns the doorknob.

***

The bell rings as Dante enters through the door, alerting Annabelle to his arrival.

'Hi Dante!' She pretends to care. 'Why are you here?'

Dante's expression shows that this is quite typical of his art dealer. 'We've got a meeting today,' he replies.

'Oh really,' Annabelle laughs.

Her quick laughter is an early sign of what becomes a long, tiresome time here at the gallery.

Dante shares his deeply held worries regarding his years with the gallery, which have left him with very little income to survive on. Dante does not stop there, explicitly opening up about having spent all of his time and money to produce the artwork they have requested, only to have it rejected.

With no sense of surprise or compassion for how this has crippled him financially, Annabelle denies all she has heard and tells a quite a different story.

This only causes Dante's frustration to worsen. 'I remember exactly what you said,' he adds, trying to keep hold of what patience he has left.

Once more, Annabelle chooses to insult the artist's intelligence.

'I still have all your emails to prove it,' Dante speaks out in frustration.

So, this is what he does: he quickly gets his phone and accesses his email account. It takes but a moment to find them. Dante reveals the emails to her, exposing her lies with her own words. He should not have been shocked by Annabelle's reaction: she simply smiles and then laughs. If such a person can live in denial even with the hard evidence of her own words in front of her, then what more can Dante do? He is powerless.

The conversation continues to drag on and Dante becomes more and more frustrated. A simple discussion about marketing and advertising his art through social media – which should have been quick and simple – has turned into a tiresome process, insulting to the artist's ego, leading to anger.

'For God's sake!' Dante cries, 'I've lost my job, I have no money, and need a fucking sale. Fucking sell my art!' he begs.

'We are getting your work out there,' Annabelle humours him.

Again, Dante tries to get through to her.

'Please,' he begs once more, 'I've done nothing but work myself to death creating all these pieces. I put in my blood, sweat and tears,' he cries, 'and what do I get?'

Staring at Annabelle, enraged that he knows how little she really cares, Dante carries on:

'A shitty, cupboard-sized flat; struggling to afford a decent, fucking shower,' Dante preaches, yelling, 'I deserve a fucking break for putting my heart and soul into this!'

Sadly, all of his crying and pleading, hoping Annabelle will acknowledge the artist's struggle, hardly fazes her into showing compassion.

'Everyone is struggling, Dante,' she says in a dull and unconvincing voice.

What is wrong with her, continuing to add salt to his open wound? Annabelle points to one of the framed art pieces displayed on the wall: a black and white photo of British supermodel Kate Moss by the artist Kate Garner. It is a stunning piece, showing the model in her Playboy Bunny suit. The surface sparkles with the diamond dust covering it. It is truly a beautiful piece in Dante's eyes.

'See this artist?' Annabella begins. 'She has a part-time job photographing the model.'

What does this have to do with me? is what is going through Dante's mind. *This person's job is photographing one of the most famous women on the planet. No doubt making fantastic money. How on earth does this even come close to my situation?*

Dante hopes that this will be the end, but Annabelle does not stop there; she points to another art piece:

'See this one?' she says. 'Had to downgrade into a one-bedroom flat so she could continue her protesting.'

Jesus Christ, how on Earth can this be any better? None of this makes anything better for Dante. *Is Annabelle mad? The photographer has a well-paid job, and the other artist chose her living accommodation.* Dante's situation isn't by choice, but the poor luck of the draw; even when he had a job, the artist could barely make enough to pay the rent.

As if things couldn't get more humiliating for the young artist:

'Look,' Annabelle says, 'I've met artists like you: all you want is fame and riches,' she preaches.

What the fuck did she just say?

'I never wanted to be famous,' he grunts, 'I just want to make a good living.'

As usual, Annabelle prattles on. Her foolish words provoke Dante even more, causing more suffering to his already fragile ego. Jesus, she would not stop! On and on she goes, telling Dante who he is and what he wants in life. Annabelle insults him even further by telling him that he wants fame and fortune. More and more, she says the complete opposite of what he has openly expressed. Oh, poor little Dante, so filled with anger towards his art dealer, who shows nothing but disrespect towards him, revealing how little she thinks of his worth.

The room starts to vibrate and blur, almost in sync with the beating of a heart. The sound of Annabelle's voice is slowly fading to mute. What is happening, he may well ask. Is Dante starting to descend into madness, or is he having some sort of anxiety attack?

'Look at her!' The Shadow Man returns, emerging behind Annabelle.

'You know what she is saying: worthless, talentless, simple-minded, a complete waste of a human being.' The sound of laughter comes from the Shadow Man, slicing into what is left of Dante's self-esteem. His laughter is high-frequency noise, becoming unbearable and too painful for Dante to bear. The artist cannot stand the cruelty of his own demon: it is too much for him now.

Then the surroundings clear and, once more, the pestering voice of his art dealer can be heard. There is nothing more Dante can do but storm out of the door.

***

Why must this torment carry on? Longing for peace and to be far away from his mental strain, walking harshly through the crowd, Dante becomes distracted by the voice of the female demon, taunting him so fiercely as he passes through the crowd. He can feel her dispiriting presence over and over as he runs head on. Dante cannot hear anything but the demon shouting, 'Loser! Loser! Loser!' over and over again. Her giggling fills the air and pushes Dante into utter despair until he can't take it anymore.

'Shut up!' he screams.

Now Dante is frozen by the glare of eyes all around him, attracting the confused attention of strangers. Not one of them is aware of Dante's personal struggles. They all look over him like vultures, wondering if he's truly lost his mind. Questions ride through the artist's mind. Is he losing his grip on sanity? All he knows is that he must get back to the station as soon as possible. Dante escapes, muttering to himself, 'Must get home... Must get home...' but such anxiety causes more unwanted stares.

***

Hours pass before Dante returns to Tower Hamlets. Instead of heading home, as he originally intended, he stops by Roman Road for a quick coffee. As closing time approaches, Dante is quietly sitting, alone, inside Café Honey, a small, vintage-style café with a pleasant atmosphere. This is exactly what Dante needs to unwind from his earlier episode.

There is hardly anyone in this café now, except for the employees: perfect for Dante. As he sits comfortably with a home-made latte, which is going down smoothly, he stares into his coffee and ponders his reflection.

His trance is interrupted by the sound of a woman's voice:

'Penny for your thoughts, tiger.'

Dante knows this voice from somewhere: a pleasant one from some recent, fond moment. Without hesitation, he lifts his head and there she is, standing in front of him. It is the red-headed woman, from the previous night. *So, this is where she works,* he guesses. How very odd that, of all the places he could have picked, he should pick the one where she works. Even in her waitress uniform, this woman is still uncannily stunning in his eyes.

'O— Hey,' he stutters with happy relief, 'it's you.'

For the first time in ages, Dante is actually happy to see someone again. The red-headed woman cannot help but smile:

'Hey, now,' she says, 'you aren't stalking me, are you?'

'Wh— No!' Dante is surprised by her witty personality. 'I just got back from a meeting at an art gallery.'

'Let me guess. Shitty day?'

Dante cannot help but chuckle. 'You could say that.'

Indeed, it is clear from the smile forming upon Dante's face that the course of his evening is changing.

The café is closing up for the night. All the tables are wiped and clean. There is the sound of chairs getting stacked up and employees finishing their tasks. The manager is counting the money and going through the receipts. The chef is in the kitchen, preparing for tomorrow's shift. Everything appears in order and the red-headed woman joins Dante. Her boss doesn't seem to mind her interaction with this young man; it is not affecting her responsibilities.

Some could mistake this for a story about potential lovebirds, so sweet and filled with smiles and laughter. The very short time that he has spent with her will become something that Dante will reminisce about from time to time. Of course, their conversation won't spark any form of romance, but the time he has spent with this red-headed woman is the happiest he's been in a while.

***

Under the night sky, Dante returns home and, for the first time in so long, he is glad to be there. A day of tragedy, which had plagued his damaged ego, can finally end with some hope. He no longer feels alone. Resting in his bed, with a smile upon his face, soon he begins to drift into the realm of slumber. Perhaps this night will be different, leaving him filled with peace and calm.

Many hours have passed, and it would seem that Mr Sandman has forgotten Dante. Guess he won't be visiting the world of dreams tonight…

As the artist lies there, his eyes open yet unaware of the room, Dante's bed starts to rock, startling him. How odd! He finds his feather-filled mattress somehow transformed into a waterbed, rolling in waves as if it were a giant block of jelly. Dante is alerted to the sudden, all-encompassing sound of 80s hard rock music. This is far beyond his control. Anxious to know the cause of such strangeness beneath him, Dante throws away his bedsheet, revealing a retro-style waterbed.

The rocking is not caused by the water, but by something else contained in the bed. Dante's eyes widen on seeing what is in his bed: a woman, the golden one from his recent dream. But how is this possible? She can breathe under water without any difficulties.

Dante is absolutely mesmerised by this familiar woman. How to react to her marvellous presence is beyond him, but the woman simply smiles and presses her soft breasts against the plastic that seals her within the mattress. The squeaking of flesh rubbing on the transparent cover is inviting and impossible to ignore. She begins to wave and mouth words as she holds herself tightly to the bed, before unexpectedly swimming away, deep into the bed, vanishing in the waters.

'Hey,' he panics, 'where did you go?'

Dante's eyes are filled with concern, trying to spot the woman and hoping she is safe. Alas, she is nowhere to be seen.

An explosion of water bursts out of the bed. Everything happens so quickly for Dante as he falls into the pierced mattress. As the panicking artist splashes in the water, the strange woman rises to accompany him.

'How's this for a wet dream?' the woman asks, speaking in the same peculiar language as his personal demons.

In a flash, the woman dunks the young artist into the waters. Dante cannot escape from her grip. The water rushes up the artist's nose, and the crashing waves of his physical struggles only panic him more. The floor is soaked by Dante's failed attempts to escape for air.

To the strange, inhuman sounds of a siren – a warning for what she has in store for Dante – the woman gracefully raises her arm, stretching those long, sharp fingernails of hers high in the air, ready to move in, to swing the into the waters...

Once again, Dante has woken up in his bed, shocked by another weird dream, filling his head with so many questions: not just about the dream, but more the strangeness of how wet he has become. No one could be this drenched just through sweating. Maybe this has been something more than just a dream.

IV

Nothing is Real

Delightful moments have filled the many days since Dante's visit to Café Honey. Now that he has someone whom he can care for – and, perhaps, who cares for him – he is no longer tormented by the clashing shackles of his own demons. The world is becoming more pleasant and brighter to live in.

At least once a week, he visits the unnamed redhead at her place of work. When it reaches closing time, Dante sits with her, as usual, and they simply chat and have coffee. Though this scene of chit-chat may not be romantic, the fact is Dante has met someone he can feel truly comfortable with. This is all he could ever have asked for. In his thoughts, the artist refers to the red-headed woman as "a rare flower"; he finds her bubbly, funny, smart, and she even has a vast knowledge of ancient culture. Of course, whether she feels the same way about him does not matter to Dante; he is just glad that has he has someone who finally acknowledges him without ulterior motive.

In time, their casual conversations progress to social outings. From peaceful walks in the scenery of Hampstead Park, their meetings move on to the intellectual and the adventurous: visits to sites of cultural heritage; exploring together the displays in the History Museum; admiring the artwork at the Tate Britain, particularly *Beata Beatrix* by Dante Gabriel Rossetti. Despite his continued struggles in finding work and selling any of his artwork, Dante is happy. The voices of his personal demons have not been heard for some time. Perhaps they are gone for good and the artist at last found peace.

Dante is now remembering the sensation of being a normal person. How sad it is that this cannot last forever. Soon Dante will have to face the harsh reality of his predicament.

***

Reading the warning letters about rent arrears, and without a reliable source of income, the pressure starts to weigh upon the young artist. Despite such recent happiness, desperation is slowly catching him up. But Dante is sensible enough to have spent the last few weeks applying for minimum wage jobs. His options are limited, yet he's smart enough to try and expand them, submitting new artwork to the Antelope Gallery and hoping that Lady Luck is on his side.

He switches on his iPad to look through his emails, scrolling down his inbox in search of the messages that he has been waiting for. It pleases him to find so many replies to his job applications. But as he stares with concentration upon the screen, an expression of disappointment soon follows: all his applications have been rejected. The more he scrolls down, the more Dante falls into a state of desperation. How can he deal with all of this? He does not know. His mind begins to unravel.

Oh, look here! Taking a deep breath, seeing that Annabelle has replied, he hopes this may bring some good news. Clicking on the link, the message opens up and Dante reads the email:

From: Annabelle Deville
Sent: 16 June 2018 16.42
To: Dante
Subject: New artwork
We are not your agent. We do not represent you. We only tried to sell your work because we felt sorry for you.
This was only a favour requested by Borat and Andy that we accepted. They both felt bad for you.
Annabelle

Felt sorry—Felt sorry for me. Me? Such antagonistic words, which fill Dante's thoughts. *How dare she—How dare they take pity upon me!* Such anger inside his head. What is more painful for Dante is that he already knew this, but never believed anyone would be cruel enough to admit it. In this state, Dante is incapable of thinking rationally. What on Earth is he going to do now? This was his last chance to turn everything around. Life really has dealt him a bad hand of cards. Now there is nothing but anxiety showing within his pupils. His savings are almost depleted, and all his remaining options have now gone down the drain. His life has gradually turned to dust, gently blown in the winds of fate.

Dante reacts like any human would: losing control with an outburst of emotional rage. He throws his iPad across the room. It hits the wall, smashing into pieces. To the sound of shattered parts scattering all over the floor, he stands still, in a state of frustration.

Dante is startled by the voice he'd hoped never to hear again.

'Another failure, it would seem.'

The Shadow Man slowly emerges into his physical form.

'Maybe it's time to come to terms with it, Dante,' whispers the Shadow Man, close behind him. 'You were born to fail,' he torments him.

'Fuck you!'

The Shadow Man cannot help but laugh, his maddening laughter surrounding Dante, piercing him like poisonous arrows.

'Shut up!' Dante cannot take the laughter any more. 'Fuck you! Fuck you all!' he screams.

Then the artist has a realisation. Even though things couldn't get any worse than this, Dante has someone he can turn to: the red-headed woman. Perhaps his friend may suggest something? She has been a burst of sunshine in his darkest times.

'You're wrong,' he says, 'I have got someone. Someone who cares about me.'

The Shadow Man cannot stop laughing.

'The redhead? Such desperation! Such false hopes!' he laughs more.

Somewhat startled by this response, confusion starts to build and rambling takes over the artist's mouth.

'W-what are you talking about?'

'Why don't you go and ask her?' the Shadow Man suggests before his body slowly begins to fade away into the air.

What did he mean? Dante puzzles. If he is ever to solve this, he will, indeed, need to go and ask the red-headed woman.

***

It is a short journey to Roman Road and the Café Honey, where Dante waits patiently. He waits and he waits, yet the red-headed woman does not show up. *How odd! This is Wednesday. This is her usual shift.* So many thoughts about where she may be, but nothing he can do but wait and hope to understand the Shadow Man's assertion.

Waiting feels like an eternity. The hour reaches close to 7:00 p.m. Soon the café will be empty after the long, busy day. Still the redhead hasn't appeared. Dante stares into his empty cup, disappointed that the Shadow Man could be on to something.

A waitress approaches, planning to wipe the surface of his table.

'Redhead?' he asks so faintly.

'Excuse me?'

'The red-headed lady,' he says. 'Is she not working today?'

The waitress lifts her cloth and looks at Dante, her face filled with curiosity.

'Wow,' she says, 'you're very chatty today.'

The artist looks at the waitress with eyes of great confusion, trying to process what the hell she's on about.

'The redhead who works here. I always talk to her. Isn't she working today?'

'I have no idea who you are talking about,' the waitress responds.

'I've been coming here for the last few weeks,' Dante persisted. 'Been meeting up with a redhead who works here.'

Now the waitress looks confused.

'No, you've been coming in, ordering a coffee and sitting right there 'til closing time.'

'No—Wait—You're wrong!' he panics, urging, 'I know she works here, and I need to see her.'

Dante's hostility starts to attract the concerned attention of the chef, who heads in his direction.

'Hi,' the chef approaches Dante. 'Do we have a problem?'

The artist's anxiety level rises as his confusion builds. Dante is forced to think back over past events. The young artist has been coming here for quite some time and meeting someone who he believed to be working here. He can't figure this out. The places they visited; the time they spent laughing together: had it all been in his head?

'I just want to see the other waitress who works here.' Dante describes her as having red hair and big blue eyes.

'No other waitress works here,' the chef says firmly, 'not one with red hair.'

This does nothing to ease Dante's confusion. Paranoia begins to invade every corner of his mind, and any rational thinking becomes lost to him.

'I know you are lying,' Dante accuses.

'I am not, sir,' the chef responds.

Dante's paranoia speaks clearly to him. It whispers ideas, making him believe that the red-headed woman has told everyone to lie for her. More and more, his suspicions grow into great doubts: perhaps she had been toying with him, just as the Shadow Man hinted, and she is trying to avoid him. Progressively, Dante's behaviour becomes unmanageable. He cannot accept any of this: that the red-headed woman was nothing but a figment of his imagination.

'Okay,' the chef says with concern, 'I think you better leave before I have to call the coppers.'

Without causing any trouble, Dante quietly leaves the café, leaving him alone with his confused thoughts.

***

The black night fills the whole sky as Dante walks through the alleyway. The artist becomes disoriented and lonely. How can he trust his thoughts or even his reality? All this time he thought he had found some form of social happiness, but it was a just a lie. Dante begins to believe that the red-headed woman was nothing but an illusion created by his mental struggles and social isolation. Or was she real and just playing him the whole time? Perhaps the artist will never know the truth. Sadly, all he can do is allow such feelings to darken his heart. Now he is truly alone…

'Alone,' the Shadow Man has returned with his familiar voice of doubt, 'abandoned, lied to by the one you cared for,' he says with amusement. 'Pathetic.'

The air is now filled with echoing laughter.

'Aw, poor little Dante,' the female demon now joins in the mockery, whispering in Dante's ear, 'always someone's bitch. Always someone's li'l plaything.' She laughs.

'Shut up,' Dante reacts.

49

The artist struggles to drown out the demons' laughter as he tries to walk away from them. Oh, why must they torment him so? His vision slowly begins to blur his surroundings, making his journey home challenging. Even the dim light from the street lamps does not help him. Could this be vertigo? Perhaps it's the effects of withdrawal. It has been a while since his last shot of heroin. The happiness he experienced over the last few weeks gave him no reason to poison himself. Or maybe this is what happens when you descend further into madness.

Sadly, his confusion will only become more difficult to resolve: his presence has attracted the attention of the local drug-dealers.

'Bro, bro,' one of the dealers approaches Dante.

Try as he might, the artist cannot get away from the dealer, who continues to follow him, pestering.

'Bro, bro,' he again harasses Dante, 'do you smoke weed?'

Frustration builds with the constant, vulture-like circling of the dealer. It doesn't matter how hard the artist tries to ignore him; this parasite will not take Dante's non-response as a hint that he is not interested. The harassment continues.

'Do you smoke weed, smoke weed, smoke weed, smoke, smoke...' he hounds Dante.

'Such a nuisance.' It is the Shadow Man. 'Wouldn't it be great if we put him outta his misery?'

Dante becomes more and more disoriented by the sound of the Shadow Man's mocking laughter.

'Stop talking!' he demands, frustrated.

The drug dealer looks with some surprise, unaware that the artist was referring, not to him, but to some demon. 'What was that?'

'Just say the word,' says the Shadow Man, continuing to whisper into Dante's ear, 'and it will be done.'

'Fuck off!' Dante reacts to the demon, wanting him to stop talking.

Dante's outburst causes the dealer to become aggressive and unstable. 'Don't tell me to fuck off!'

Whether through lack of maturity or dependency on drugs, the dealer is becoming more emotional and hostile. His outburst acts like a beacon, alerting his drug-dealing friends nearby, who, one by one, emerge from the shadows. Dante's situation is starting to look bleak.

'This li'l gay-boy wants to start something.'

Dante tries to explain that he wasn't talking to the dealer. 'No, I wa—'

But one of the dealers pushes the artist against the wall.

'Please stop!' Dante begs, 'You don't have to do this.'

But these insignificant criminals are unwilling to be civil and allow Dante to explain. The artist is unable to escape as they barricade him against a wall.

Dante's blurred vision makes it difficult for him to focus. He struggles to take in the reality of his situation, outnumbered and outmatched, and is helpless to fight back as the gang start to push him around, trying to provoke the unfortunate soul.

One of the aggressors throws a swinging punch to Dante's abdomen, winding him. Many others follow. He receives a blow to the face and falls to the ground, where, helpless, he endures the onslaught of feet and fists to his body.

'Just say the word...'

The Shadow Man stands over the artist, watching him so calmly as he is beaten to a pulp.

'Shut up!' Dante snaps, as trainers continue to rain down with force on his face and ribs. 'You're not real!'

The Shadow Man continues to stand over Dante, unaffected by the pummelling that the artist is receiving.

'Who said we aren't real?'

'What did you say?'

As rapid fists and soles of trainers continue to make contact, Dante thinks this will be his end. All goes dark...

The shroud of darkness is the least of Dante's worries. He hears unexpected cries from his attackers: the horrifying sound of bones crushing and guts splatting. Still in darkness, Dante is unaware of the cause of these sounds; sounds of a fate worse that his own.

As his eyes regain their sight, Dante is frozen in horror at the dreadful scene: the display of human entrails scattered all over the ground. In the centre of this bloodbath, trembling, Dante cautiously looks down at his hands and, slowly lifting them, sees that his palms are soaked in the blood of his attackers. Dante shakes uncontrollably, paralysed with fear. This sight is too gruesome even for someone with a full grip on their sanity.

He knows that he cannot stay and be accused. He wants to get up; he wants to run away, but he is too scare to try. Dante knows that someone or something is watching him. Its features are clouded in shadow; only its piercing, glowing eyes identify this unholy abomination. Dante does not know what to do; he is far too scared even to breathe.

Worse still are the strange sounds: some eerie clicking, almost howling noises that Dante cannot identify. He hopes this is nothing but some twisted dream he is having. All he can do is close his eyes and let tears run down his bloody face, praying, *if this is the end, let it be quick...*

V

Gorgeous Nightmare

Never before in his life had such a moment left Dante this broken. He is now alone and beaten in both mind and body, with no spirit left to go on. The sound of the door creaking open signals his return to his gloomy home. Now nothing but a ghostly figure hidden in the darkness, he slowly heads towards the bathroom.

The moment the light is switched on, his face is revealed in the mirror: battered, bruised and bloody. Slowly, he turns the screeching tap and water flows into the sink as he prepares to clean his face. His hands scoop the surface of clear water, splashing it onto the dried blood over and over, and soon the ripples in the sink turn red. Dante's face, clean at last, reveals the cuts and bruises left by the victims of his demon.

Slowly, as he walks into the bedsit, the only thought going through Dante's mind is the need to break the silence of his loneliness. Carefully, the artist takes out a vinyl record from his music collection and slowly places it on the portable player. Once the record starts spinning, the sound of his favourite jazz performer begins. Dante sits in front of the mirror, listening to Collette giving her introduction before the rest of the band follows her raw talent. The lonely stare of his reflection reveals the face of someone who has fallen so low.

Displayed on the desk beside Dante is a small tub. Slowly, he removes the lid, revealing untouched white paint. Gently, he places his fingers into the liquid, scooping it out and smearing it onto his face until he resembles a white ghost. Broken to the point of madness, he manically laughs to his reflection. Once the white paint has dried, Dante starts to apply others to his skin. A series of many colours begins to cover his face until he is nothing but a clown.

The room is ready, and in Dante's mind the stage is now set. He stands in the centre and, as the music begins to build, his body moves to its rhythms. As the music progresses, Dante moves more animatedly: waving his arms and hips, entwined with the sound of Collette's vocals, lost in a trance, spinning himself around like a ballerina. In his mind, he is performing in front of a large audience inside a theatre.

Soon, his movements become chaotic: swinging around like a flying banshee, aggressively grabbing a painting near him and destroying it by throwing it violently onto the ground. The emotional artist does not stop, continuing to dance and destroy as much of his artwork as possible, kicking his foot through the canvas. But it is not just one, nor even two, but all of them. His feet and arms have become instruments of destruction upon his failures. He turns to the blade of a knife, tearing a horizontal line in each remaining canvas until there are no more.

In this moment, upon the death of his art, his effort turns to exhaustion and Dante knows he should rest. His dramatic performance has caused the paint to run down his face. Now he sits on the tattered couch. Silent and broken to the point of spiritual emptiness, he resembles a living corpse.

'Pathetic.'

The Shadow Man stands behind Dante. This cannot be just in his mind, a manifestation of his madness. Has he come to finish him, as he did those dealers? Oh, sweet Dante, praying that he will be released from his mortal suffering...

The sound of a woman's giggle breaks his thoughts away from his could-be end:

'Hmmm,' hums the familiar voice. 'Aw, don't pay any attention to him.' It speaks so sexily.

Dante turns to the left, following the voice, to reveal the speaker, on her hands and knees like an animal, next to him on the couch. It is one of the twins from his dream. Her presence is far too much for Dante. How can she be here?

Suddenly, his face is moved away by a strange, scaly hand.

'He's always been a bit of a sour-puss.' The owner of the hand is revealed as the other twin, who thrusts her large, perfect breasts towards Dante's eyes, an image that he finds inescapable.

'Hmmm,' her sister giggles, 'he likes what he sees, huh!' She crawls closer to Dante, her strange, inhuman hand slowly reaching towards his crotch, gently touching and caressing his private part. 'Hmmm,' she giggles. 'Oh wow!'

'He's so big, dear sister,' her twin says playfully, teasing the other, 'I'm getting excited just thinking about it.'

'No fair, sister! You're having all the fun,' she moans so sensually.

Her sister responds, slowly reaching towards the breasts of her sibling, squeezing them firmly just to excite her. Soon they begin to tease poor Dante, both so uncontrollably aroused that they cannot hesitate for their lips to touch and their tongues tangle together in incest.

Dante manages to look away with eyes of hopelessness.

'Am I— This must be a nightmare,' he thinks out loud.

But this surreal moment feels beyond the realm of dreams, something Dante cannot wake up from.

'Hmmm,' – arms that are quite familiar wrap around Dante – 'then I must be your gorgeous nightmare.'

The artist recognises the golden woman with whom he has engaged in sexual intercourse once before.

The twin on Dante's right slowly lifts her leg and places herself on top of his lap. Her eyes lock on to the artist, smiling with the motive of sinister seduction. Gently, the bald humanoid holds on to him, her body close to his. Her breasts squish upon Dante's face. He is helpless and powerless to do anything as, breathing heavily and giggling, she rubs herself upon the tormented artist. She now passionately locks lips with his, while her sister, at the same time, starts to unzip his jeans and reach to touch his manhood.

'Hmmm,' Gorgeous Nightmare, aroused, hums to the twins, 'he's so good, isn't he!'

She places small intimate kisses upon Dante's cheek, desperately wanting him like before.

'Why do you torment me so?' Dante asks them.

One of the twins eases his face to hers as she gives him a look of sincerity. 'Torment you?'

'We love you, Dante,' her sister continues.

'And we want to stay with you forever and ever and ever,' Gorgeous Nightmare joins them in saying.

Slowly and gently, the twin on top kisses him while the other caresses him. Dante does not fight back, not wanting them to stop.

Dante's eyes catch sight of a surviving blank canvas.

Gorgeous Nightmare, noticing Dante's stare, begins to smile.

'Last canvas.' She points to it. 'What will your masterpiece be?'

The Shadow Man and his female counterpart emerge next to the canvas. The demons multiply before Dante's eyes.

'Pathetic! Worthless! Talentless!'

'I am no good,' Dante agrees, full of self-doubt.

'Hmmm, no good?' Gorgeous Nightmare responds gently. 'Why? Because they said so? Perhaps you need to remember why you wanted to become an artist in the first place.'

'A time when you were happy?' suggests one of the twins.

Dante asks himself a question he has never asked before: *When I was happy?*

From somewhere deep within, Dante recalls memories of a life long ago: when he was that child in the room with the red carpet, happy and filled with passion, before the world crushed him of his talent; before those around him took advantage of his gifts; long ago, before he was chewed up, spat out, and looked upon as needing charity. Pleasant memories, long forgotten, slowly move on to heavenly images of the red-headed woman.

'No,' Gorgeous Nightmare interrupts, 'do not think of her.'

'She abandoned you and toyed with you', one of the twins continues.

'Perhaps you should paint us,' the other one suggests, sexually.

'Why do you care so much?' Dante asks.

Gorgeous Nightmare slowly licks his cheek. 'It is because we love you.'

'We need you,' one of the twins carries on.

Her words create further confusion upon Dante's face.

'Why me?' he adds, faintly. 'I'm a nobody,' he labels himself.

Once again, Gorgeous Nightmare takes an interest, placing her claw-like hand underneath Dante's chin, looking at him with eyes full of confidence for the artist.

'Because the talents you have are a gift from the gods,' she responds.

His eyes look away from these inhuman women. Why him? Dante is puzzled. They could easily select a more successful artist.

'I don't understand,' he says.

'You're destined for great things,' answers one of the twins.

'Great things?' he repeats, turning to face her.

All three look at him with confidence in his ability to meet their high expectations.

'It is inevitable,' confirms the other twin.

Now they are hoping that Dante will finally embrace them, hoping he will submit to them. Slowly, he starts to give in, no longer resisting their need for his lips to touch theirs. So now his flesh, his body, burn for their pleasure and their animal lust can finally be fulfilled. The three strange women of inhuman origin climb over Dante, ready to consume him with their untamed hunger.

Now is the time for Dante. He squeezes oil paints from their tubes onto the pallet and swirls a paintbrush in a glass of paint thinner. His eyes stare into the blank canvas. Now, at last, he paints. To the melody of the brush colliding with the surface, Dante is doing something he has never done before: he is smiling, happy to be painting.

His moment of passion begins to reignite the flames he once lost. As they begin to feel his re-lit spark, one by one, his demons slowly vanish into the ether.

Now comes the finishing touch of the brush. At last, the painting is complete. For the first time in so long, Dante has finished a painting that has left him fulfilled.

'It's beautiful,' a familiar voice praises, breaking the silence of Dante's concentration.

It's a voice the artist was not expecting to hear again. He turns and, to his surprise, there she is, standing in plain sight: the red-headed woman.

'I'm so sorry for letting things end in that way,' she apologises. 'I wanted to see you so much, but they knew— They knew I would start to get in the way.'

Dante looks at her, his eyes filled with questions.

'How did y— Wait! What do you mean by them?' he asks.

Just before the red-headed woman can begin to explain, Dante notices something else quite out of the ordinary.

'Wait! How can this be?' He is looking through the window. 'It is still night.'

Dante has been painting for hours and yet time has not passed. It should have been morning by now.

He finds no answers by staring at his reflection. Turning around to see what is behind him brings a further riddle: Dante sees himself on the couch, wearing the clothes he wore the day he lost his job. How can he be there? Looking more closely at his other self, he understands: the needle in his arm and the discolouring to his face; it is obvious that he has overdosed.

'I'm dead, aren't I?'

Finally, he has created a masterpiece and now no-one will be able to appreciate it.

'Typical,' he says, 'just fucking typical!'

'No Dante,' the red-headed woman responds, 'they won't let you die.'

Questions that Dante cannot answer, he now begins to ask of her. Why is this happening to him? Who are these strange beings from his dreams? And, finally, what does all of this mean? The red-headed woman is happy to explain, revealing Dante's role in this shocking scene. In the end, however, it will make no difference; the artist will retain no memory of what has transpired.

The one question Dante should have asked from the very beginning, he now voices:

'Who are you? 'At least tell me your name.'

'Beatrice.'

At last, after waiting for so long, her name is revealed.

The front door suddenly opens, revealing a glow of white light. Beatrice walks towards it.

'No, wait!' He tries to stop her. 'Ar-are you some kind of guardian angel?'

Beatrice turns to him.

'You remind me so much of him,' she says.

'Who?' he asks and stands there so confused and yet more curious about what she means.

'Dante,' she smiles, 'my Dante.'

She leaves the artist, slowly walking through the open door. Her departure causes the troubled artist to panic.

'No, please don't go!' he begs.

Dante runs as fast as he can, trying to reach the door, hoping to stop Beatrice, but he is thwarted by a sudden, blinding white light.

***

There is a loud, then low sound of static shock as Dante's heart is revived. He responds in a state of disorientation, unaware of what is happening before his wide, panicked eyes. Now he has to return to the living.

'Can you hear me?' a female paramedic asks. 'Do you know who you are? Do you know where you are?'

Dante is blinded by the waves of the tiny light used by the paramedic to assess the responsiveness of his pupils.

'The patient is male,' the female paramedic identifies, 'Caucasian, early 30s, subject to accidental overdose. Patient needs to be taken into emergency care immediately.'

Dante, now revived and carried away, is placed in the back of the ambulance outside. The back doors are closed, and the vehicle driven to the nearest hospital.

The remaining paramedics are gathering their equipment until…

'Sweet Jesus!' The reaction of one paramedic to what he sees in front of him.

His expression, as he stares at the recently finished painting, is the same one that Dante had produced within his realm between life and death. 'Hey, Phil!' he calls out. 'You gotta check this out.'

Phil responds to his colleague's call with curiosity and approaches him.

'Wow!' he reacts. 'What do you make of it?'

Neither can help but be drawn to what is in front of them, overwhelmed by the impact of Dante's artwork.

'I don't know,' his colleague replies, 'but I just can't take my eyes off it.'

As Dante is rushed into emergency care, the last remaining paramedics at his flat cannot help themselves; they continue to stare, amazed and entranced by the portrait of Gorgeous Nightmare. Their eyes are the first of many that will witness the genius they will come to know as Dante.

Epilogue

Two months have passed since Dante's encounter with death. Sunlight hits the City of London, causing it to glow, to appear a place of wonders. For many, this is a city where dreams are made.

Now we view the space within the FKH gallery, located in Marylebone High Street. This is where dreams can come true for artists. The walls within the gallery now exhibit what will soon be revealed to the world.

Once glimpsed, no one can resist the urge to stop and stare. There, at last, the space is filled with a series of paintings by Dante. Each painting is a portrait, a tribute to those inhuman beings now revealed to this world. And these are not paintings to be ignored. So now, surrounded by artwork of such divine eerie force, Adrian Reeves – the curator – is dazzled. How could he possibly look away from this mesmerizing collection? It is amazing that a simple layer of paint covering the surface of stretched cotton can draw the eye, satisfying even the most narcissistic nature.

Adrian's concentrated admiration is broken by the echoes of footsteps, growing louder to reveal who is approaching. It is Dante.

Our tragic protagonist has transformed: his face is healthy and full of colour; his clothes appear to be new and expensive. Clearly, his brush with death has had a miraculous effect and forever changed his life. The artist is now full of confidence and no longer in need of drugs. He is a completely new man.

'Dante!' Adrian expresses such joy. 'Glad you've made it,' he says. 'How've you been, my friend?'

'Same old, same old.'

How unlike our character. So calm and well-balanced, not even a hint of foul temper or insecurity. Adrian, so pleased that he has shown up – even though Dante's arrival was planned – is ready to discuss the development of the upcoming show.

'I just can't keep my eyes away from any of them, mate!' Adrian is full of praise.

The curator turns his attention to the *Gorgeous Nightmare* painting.

'I dunno know what it is,' he says, 'but it's almost like they are calling for me.' He continues, 'I just fucking love them!'

Dante has no memory of what transpired during his near-death experience, yet he believes that his artwork came from somewhere far beyond his imagination.

'This show is going to be a major hit,' Adrian gushes. 'You're going to be a star!' he carries on. 'Got a name for the show yet?'

It is at this moment that it is revealed from Dante's mouth: 'Elseland.'

What a name! Trivial within the limits of the human language. How amusing! Its true name is nothing any living organism is capable of comprehending: the name of my home that no tongue can pronounce.

Now we have reached the point where you assume this is a happy ending for our dear Dante.

Unfortunate for you, then, that the wheels of fate are set in motion. Sadly, I'm afraid this isn't the end of the story. Nor this can be called a story, more a warning of what is coming for you all. This is neither a beginning nor an end, but once you have finished these words…

My brave reader, this is where the story truly begins.